Weekly Reader Books presents

THE UNDERCOVER KIDS

Mary Blount Christian
Illustrated by Don Madden

TWO BOOKS INSIDE:

The Two-Ton Secret
and
The Undercover Kids and The Museum Mystery

Albert Whitman & Company

This book is a presentation of Weekly Reader Books. Weekly Reader Books offers book clubs for children from preschool through high school. For further information write to: **Weekly Reader Books,** 4343 Equity Drive, Columbus, Ohio 43228.

Two-Ton Secret is published by arrangement with Albert Whitman & Company. **The Undercover Kids and the Museum Mystery** is edited by Weekly Reader Books and published by arrangement with Albert Whitman & Company.

TWO-TON SECRET

To my friends at Valley Oaks Elementary

Library of Congress Cataloging in Publication Data

Christian, Mary Blount.
Two-ton secret.

(First read-alone mysteries)
SUMMARY: Ace crime-solvers Deke and Snitch track down a bulldozer that is missing from a local construction site.
[1. Mystery and detective stories] I. Madden, Don, 1927–   II. Title.
PZ7.C4528Tw   [E]   81-346
ISBN 0-8075-8165-8   AACR1

THE UNDERCOVER KIDS
AND THE MUSEUM MYSTERY

Remembering Julian Blount and Louise Blount Brown

Library of Congress Cataloging in Publication Data

Christian, Mary Blount.
   The undercover kids and the museum mystery.

   Summary: Deke and Snitch find out who's stealing priceless relics from the Egyptian exhibit at the museum.
   I. [Mystery and detective stories] I. Madden, Don, 1927– ill. II. Title.
PZ7.C4528Un 1983   [E]   83-16682
ISBN 0-8075-8302-2

TWO-TON SECRET

I wiped the paint off my arm and
looked at my new sign.

My friend Snitch read the sign.
He pulled his ear. He always pulls
his ear when he's upset.

"What's wrong?" I asked.

"I see your name, but where's mine?"

"You're the associate," I said.

"What's that?"

"That means you can be the boss when I'm not here," I explained.

"Oh," Snitch said. He pulled his ear again. "What expenses?"

"Oh, you know," I said, "a soda pop or some raisin cookies. We might have to eat on the job."

Snitch looked happier. He likes raisin cookies.

Suddenly tires squealed. A truck
skidded up to the curb. "Drake Road
Construction Company" was printed
on the door.

"Don't look now," I told Snitch. "But a man with a hard hat is getting out of that truck."

Snitch looked. He always looks when I tell him not to.

The man came over to us. "Is this sign true?" he asked. "Are you detectives?"

"Deke King and Associate," I said. "We never lie."

The man scratched his head. "Do you know where Three-Mile Road and Frontage Road meet?" he asked.

"About a mile from here," I said. "Maybe ten, fifteen minutes by bike."

He nodded. "I'm doing some road construction work there. If you want a job, meet me at the crossing in an hour. By the way, my name's Drake."

He turned and headed back to his truck. I heard him mutter, "Why I'm doing this I don't know."

"A good undercover detective never looks like a detective," I told my associate. "We'll need disguises. See what you can dig up at your house."

I dashed up to my bedroom and looked through my secret trunk. I found a pair of phony glasses with a nose and moustache attached. I put them on and grabbed my notebook and pencil.

When I got back to the front yard,
Snitch was waiting for me. He had a
patch over one eye.

"For crying out loud!" I shouted.
"A pirate outfit?"

He shrugged. "It was the best I could
do," he said. At least, he'd found a
magnifying glass and some face powder
in case we needed fingerprints.

We rode our bikes to Frontage and
Three-Mile roads. At the crossing
was a fenced-in area. A bulldozer,
a shed, and a pile of dirt were inside.

The man, Mr. Drake, greeted us. He
looked at my false nose and Snitch's
patch. "Maybe this is a mistake," he
said. "If anybody finds out —"

"No one will suspect a thing," I said,
to make him feel better. "Now what's
the problem?"

"Thieves keep stealing my bulldozers,"
he said. "The police can't find any
clues, and I can't afford to lose any
more machines."

15

I flipped through my notebook for an empty page. Snitch started throwing face powder on everything in sight.

"How can thieves steal the 'dozers without anybody noticing?" I asked.

"They come at night, when no one's around," Mr. Drake said. "For a while I took a wheel off each bulldozer at night. I figured the thieves couldn't roll away one of these two-ton babies with a missing wheel."

"But they did?" I asked, scribbling in my notebook.

16

He nodded. "They must have brought their own wheels. After that, I started taking out the spark plugs and ignitions at night. But the thieves just used their own parts to get the machines going."

He sighed. "Once they even brought a flatbed truck to carry a 'dozer away. I could tell from the tire tracks."

Snitch whistled. "Wasn't that expensive?"

Mr. Drake nodded. "Sure, but a hot 'dozer sells for $10,000 or more."

It was *my* turn to whistle. That was a lot of money for a few hours' work.

"Hmmm," I said. "Aren't stolen 'dozers easy to spot? Don't they have serial numbers, like bicycles?"

Mr. Drake shrugged. "The numbers scratch off easily. And most bulldozers are yellow. A stolen one is lost in the batch—like a tree in the forest."

Snitch was climbing up the dirt pile.
Suddenly he whooped and slid down. He
looked silly for an undercover
detective.

Then I thought, why not? If anyone was
watching, we'd look like ordinary kids
playing in the dirt.

I climbed up the pile and slid to the
bottom. The dirt felt cool and loose
and fresh.

"Did someone just dump this dirt?" I asked Mr. Drake.

"No," he said. "All the dirt on the lot's been here for weeks. We brought it in when we started the road work."

I scratched my chin. Odd, I thought. Dirt that had been here so long should be packed solid. I poked my finger into it. A few inches below the surface, the earth was hard.

Someone had dumped fresh dirt on top of the old pile!

"How many tractors have you lost?" I asked Mr. Drake.

"Five so far," he answered.

"Why do you think we can find those 'dozers if the police can't?" I asked.

Mr. Drake's shoulders drooped. "I don't know. But I'll try anything."

"Ummm," I said. "And when was the last 'dozer stolen?"

"Last night," he said. "I put up this
wire fence a week ago. I thought it
would keep the thieves from stealing
the machines. But this morning a 'dozer
was gone, and the gate to the fence was
still locked."

He shook his head. "How could anyone
steal a two-ton tractor through a locked
fence? And why would someone steal just
one tractor and leave another one behind?"

I wondered, too. Maybe the fence had
been cut. I sent my associate to check it.

Meanwhile, I walked around to the back
of the shed. The ground there was loose,
like the top of the dirt pile. Had the
thieves brought in the dirt to hide
the evidence?

Clues:
1. Loose dirt behind the shed and on the dirt pile
2. No cut marks anywhere on the fence
3. Locked gate
4. Bulldozer left behind

Snitch reported there were no cut marks anywhere on the fence.

I stared at the list of clues: loose dirt behind the shed and on the dirt pile; no cut marks anywhere on the fence; locked gate; bulldozer left behind.

The answer had to be right in front of me. Nobody could take the bulldozer without breaking through the fence. The 'dozer must still be on the construction site—hidden somewhere.

"One more question, sir," I said. "Will you take the fence with you when this job is finished?"

"Of course," he said. "Why?"

That was all I needed to know. I stood tall.

"Because I think the answer, sir, is right under our noses. Your bulldozer hasn't been stolen!"

"What!" he shouted. "I should have known better than to hire two kids!"

I ignored him. "Do you have a metal detector, sir?" I asked.

"Of course. We use it to find
underground pipes and cables,"
he said.

He got the detector and turned
it on. It hummed quietly.

"Now put it over the ground behind
the shed," I said.

The detector crackled like crazy.

"Your bulldozer's buried right here,"
I shouted.

Snitch sprinkled some powder on the
ground, as if fingerprints would show
up there. He yanked at his ear.

"It all adds up," I told Mr. Drake.
"The thieves climb the fence. They use
one of your 'dozers to dig a hole. Then
they bury the other 'dozer."

I stood taller. "That explains why they left
one tractor behind. They throw the
extra dirt on your pile, hiding the
evidence in front of you.

"When you finish the job," I went on,
"you take up the fence. Then the thieves
return and dig up the 'dozer."

Snitch and I stood back while Mr. Drake shoveled dirt from the ground. Sure enough, there was the 'dozer, all wrapped up in plastic.

Snitch even managed to get a fingerprint off the machine. It was his own, of course.

"That's why I'm the boss and you're the associate," I told him.

Mr. Drake called the police right away. They told him they'd stake out the road crossing after the construction work was done. The thieves would fall right into their hands.

Mr. Drake said after this he'd paint
his equipment green with pink polka
dots. He figured stolen machines would
be easier to spot that way.

He paid us two days' pay instead of one.
I guess he figured we were twice as smart
as the police who'd been on the case.

We couldn't argue with that. He'd hired
the best Undercover Kids in the business —
Deke King and Associate.

The Undercover Kids and THE Museum Mystery

I turned the piggy bank upside down and shook it. Two quarters clattered to the sidewalk. I shook again. Nothing more came out.

Snitch tugged at his ear. He always tugs at his ear when he's worried. "That's it? Two quarters?"

I nodded. Business had been bad lately. Snitch and I hadn't had a mystery to solve in weeks.

Snitch grabbed the newspaper. "Maybe there's something in here. You know, 'Jewels Stolen, Reward Given'—that sort of thing."

I spotted an interesting article on the front page. "Hey," I said. "An Egyptian exhibit is opening this weekend at the museum."

Snitch pulled his ear. "You mean with a dead mummy and stuff like that? Ickh!"

I shrugged. "I guess. Maybe gold and precious jewels, too."

I had an idea. I looked for some paper and a pencil. All I could find were my arithmetic homework and a crayon. They would have to do.

I cut the paper into a small rectangle, about the size of a billfold. On the blank side I wrote:

MYSTERIES SOLVED
NO CASE TOO HARD
$1.00 A DAY
PLUS EXPENSES
DEKE KING AND ASSOCIATE...
THE UNDERCOVER KIDS

"That exhibit will attract crooks," I explained to my partner. "The museum will need expert protection."

"Right!" Snitch agreed. "I wonder who they'll get!"

"Us!" I yelled. "We are the experts in this town, aren't we?"

I hopped on my bike. "The news story said the director's name is Dudley Dover. That's who we have to see."

Snitch hopped on his bike and followed me.

A panel truck was parked outside the museum. Some men in white coveralls were taking carved pedestals from the truck into the museum. "Acme Display Aids" was printed on the backs of their coveralls.

"They must be delivering stuff for the
Egyptian show," I said to Snitch.

I spotted a man in a dark three-piece suit and wire-rim glasses. He stood with his arms folded, watching the workers. I could tell he was the director, Dudley Dover. Directors don't have to work. They just give orders and watch.

I handed him my business card. He stared at it. "Ninety-five minus six isn't eighty-six," he said.

He was reading the wrong side of my ad. I blushed. "My teacher agrees with you, sir. The other side, please."

He turned the paper over. "I don't need any detectives," he said, "but your rates are reasonable. Help those men carry in the pedestals and I'll pay you a dollar."

Money is money, I figured. I got Snitch and
told him to grab one end of a big pedestal.

"What're you kids doin'?" one of the
workers snarled.

"I told them to help," Dudley Dover said.
"It's taking you men forever."

The worker grumbled and glared at us. But
he didn't argue with the director.

Snitch and I grabbed a pedestal and carried it into the museum. It was really lightweight. I could practically have carried it myself.

We worked the rest of the afternoon. Dudley Dover paid us our dollar and we left.

The next day we went to see the exhibit. There were all kinds of statues and gold bowls and headdresses and stuff like that.

A guard stood at the entrance to the exhibit. The museum seemed pretty safe without our help. So you can imagine my surprise when I got a call from the director the next morning.

"Half the exhibit is gone!" he shouted. "The museum doors were locked last night, and the alarms didn't go off. But some of the statues and jewels disappeared! If I don't get them back, I'll be fired."

"Say no more," I said. "The Undercover Kids will be there in a jiffy."

I called Snitch. I told him to get into a disguise, like a mummy costume or something. I figured we could hang around the museum. Maybe the crooks would come back for the rest of the stuff.

I got out the first-aid kit and wrapped myself up with gauze. Then I pedaled to the museum no-handed.

Snitch met me there. He was dressed in a polka dot dress, high heels, and a crazy hat.

"For crying out loud!" I shouted. "Are you bananas? What are you doing in that polka dot dress and crazy hat? Do you think Egyptian mummies wore stuff like that?"

"*Mummy?*" Snitch asked, tugging at his ear. "I thought you said *Mommy!*"

"Never mind," I said. "Let's go inside. Er, walk a little behind me, will you? I'm embarrassed to be seen with you."

Snitch glared at me. "Well, you look like an escapee from a first-aid course."

I shrugged off his insult. I stalked to the room where the Egyptian exhibit was.

Sure enough, there were some empty pedestals where the statues and jewels had been. The guard wasn't there. He must have been on a break.

A man came into the room after us.

"Walk around and pretend to look at the exhibit," I whispered to Snitch.

He hobbled over in his mother's heels and stared at a statue in the shape of a cat.

The man followed Snitch around the room.
He stopped at each display. He looked kind
of familiar. Then a piece of gauze flapped
over my eyes and I couldn't see.

I blew—*ptiuu, ptiuu*—to move the piece of
gauze up. But it kept flapping back.
Suddenly I heard a sound—
SCHLUUUUMP!

I blew again and the gauze moved. I
couldn't believe what I saw. The cat statue
was gone, and the man was walking toward
the door.

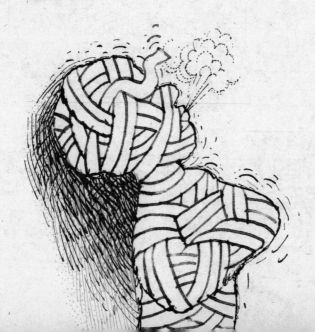

There were only three of us in the room.
Snitch and I didn't have the cat. The man
had to have it.

"Grab him!" I yelled. "Don't let him get away!"

The guard came running into the room. He and Snitch and I tackled the man. We all fell to the floor.

The man yelled something angry—something I won't repeat.

Just then Dudley Dover came into the room. I told him what had happened—how the cat was there and then suddenly not there.

The guard and Dudley Dover searched the man. They couldn't find the cat.

"I just wanted to see the exhibit," the man said. "I got curious when I helped bring in the pedestals and things."

I knew I'd seen the man before. He was one of the movers I'd helped.

"Wouldn't you like me to take the empty pedestals out?" the man asked Dudley Dover.

The director sighed. "Yes, that's a good idea. The boys will help you move them. Bring your truck around to the back of the museum."

The man brought his truck around. "You don't have to help," he told us.

"We'd like to," I said. We could use the dollar Dudley Dover would give us.

I unwrapped what was left of my gauze.
Then Snitch and I grabbed different sides
of a pedestal. We struggled under its
weight.

"I must be getting weak," Snitch said. "I
didn't have this much trouble before. Did
you?"

"Naw," I answered, puffing. "I guess it's
because we haven't eaten."

The man looked as if he was struggling
with his pedestal, too.

I frowned, thinking.

I went over the clues in my head. The
artifacts were there on display in plain sight.
Then they were gone. The museum doors
were locked overnight, and the alarms
didn't go off. No one was seen carrying
anything out. And a statue of a cat was
stolen right before my eyes—bandaged as
they were.

I had to think harder. The Undercover
Kids' reputation was at stake.

First the pedestals were light, then they
were heavy.

Suddenly it dawned on me. The artifacts hadn't been stolen at all—at least, not last night or this morning. They were being stolen right now. And the Undercover Kids were helping!

"Put the pedestal down," I told Snitch, "and get the director quick. I've solved the case."

Snitch looked puzzled. But he ran off and came back with the director and the guard.

"What's all this about?" Dudley Dover asked. "You say you've found the artifacts? Where?"

"I realized something was wrong," I said, "when the pedestals were light when we carried them in and heavy when we carried them out. My guess is, the top of this pedestal is a trapdoor."

I felt around, pushing and pulling on the
scrollwork. I figured I'd find a button there
somewhere.

Suddenly the top of the pedestal opened. Inside was the statue of the cat. The pedestal was hollow and lined with straw.

"That explains the funny schluuping noise," I said. "The man passed by and pushed the button and the pedestal just swallowed the cat up."

Dudley Dover said, "Boys, you'll never know how much I appreciate your help. Why, I'll recommend you to all my friends!"

Snitch elbowed me.

"That's fine, sir," I said. "But you owe us a dollar for the day."

I decided not to charge him for the gauze. After all, the publicity we got was worth something. The newspaper headline the next day read: